I LOVE YOU MORE THAN CEREAL

Maeva and Dad Redefine Love

Justin & Alexis Black

Illustrated Author photo: Leah Simone Feimster
Photographer, Patty Leonor Photography, Pattyleonor.com

First Edition Book, April 2023

Book cover design, illustration, editing, and interior layout by:

www.1000storybooks.com

DEDICATION

To our daughter, Maeva Rose Black, and all the other kids on a lifelong journey to love themselves and others. The world will want to give you its meaning of love, but you and your family get to redefine that every day.

I love YOU more than cereal!

T🥣: _____

FROM: _____

Maeva ran in while her dad was pouring their favorite bowl of cereal.

"Daddy! Daddy! Guess what?"

"What is it, Maeva?"

"I love the new bike you and Mommy bought me!

Thank you, Mommy & Daddy!"

"Of course, sweetheart!"

"I love the color!" Maeva said excitedly. "The purple makes it stand out from every other bike!

I love the wheels! They're big and round like the moon and shiny like the sun. And I also love my super wheels on the side, too!"

"Do you mean your training wheels?" Dad asked.

Maeva nodded. "Yeah, those things!"

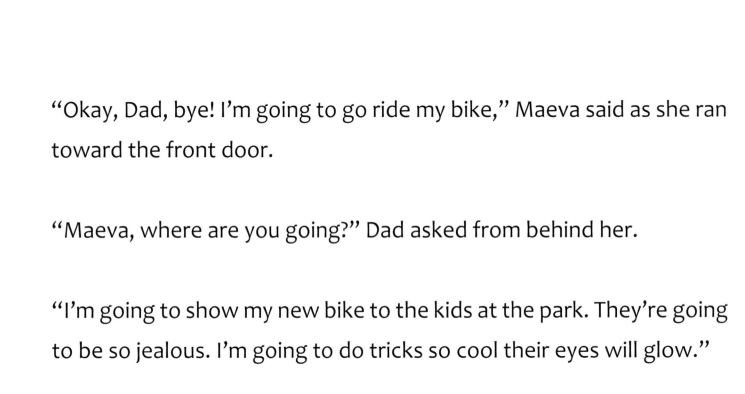

"Okay, Dad, bye! I'm going to go ride my bike," Maeva said as she ran toward the front door.

"Maeva, where are you going?" Dad asked from behind her.

"I'm going to show my new bike to the kids at the park. They're going to be so jealous. I'm going to do tricks so cool their eyes will glow."

"I'll do front flips, back flips, and jump as high as the stars! I'll ride so fast the other kids will eat my dust.

I'm going to honk my horn so loud their ears will ring like school bells.

Then, while they're admiring my bike, I'm going to pull out all the candy I love and **NOT** share any of it! Just like they did to me last weekend.

Then I'll come home happy."

"Wow," Dad said with big eyes. "That's pretty well thought out."

"Yup, and I have no time to waste, so see ya, Dad!" Maeva turned to run out the door.

"Wait one second, little lady!" Dad said. "Can I ask a question before you go?"

Maeva stopped with a nod.

"You used the word 'love' quite a bit when you were talking about your bike," he said. "What does 'love' mean to you?"

Maeva scratched her head as she thought. "I think it means to feel really, really, really good, right?

Or like how I feel when I see the color purple, or eat my favorite bowl of cereal! Or how I'll feel when the other kids are jealous of my new bike."

"Oh, Maeva… what if I told you that love isn't only how we *feel*, but it's about how we treat ourselves and other people too? Love is also what we *do*," Dad said.

"You can *feel* love for your bike, but *loving* your bike means you'll choose to take care of it."

"Like when I spilled my cereal milk all over the table and Mommy helped me clean it up!" Maeva said. "I was scared she'd be mad, but she was patient."

That's because Mommy's love helps her be patient. How does it *feel* when Mommy's love is patient with you?" Dad said.

Maeva responded, "It makes me feel warm and happy."

Daddy nodded his head in agreement.

"And love doesn't get upset right away. Does that mean love doesn't brag either, Daddy?"

"That's right, honey. Love doesn't brag to make others feel bad. What else can you think of?" Dad asked.

"Love means forgiving others and not keeping a list of their mistakes like Mommy did with me."

"Exactly," Dad said. "Love isn't selfish. Love always protects, always trusts, always hopes. And, last but not least," Dad added, "love never fails."

"Like how you and Mommy will never stop loving me, no matter what I do!"

"But Dad! What about when other kids aren't kind to me? What about when they brag in front of me or when they're selfish? What happens when they don't love *me*?"

"That's the thing about love, Maeva," Dad said. "It doesn't wait until everyone else deserves it. If we love others only when they are deserving, then who would ever be loved?"

"I guess you and Mommy do love me even when I'm not the nicest," Maeva remembered suddenly.

Dad considered how to best explain it. "Do I share my hot wings with you, even when I'm down to my last one?"

Maeva nodded. "Well, yeah, of course!"

"Sharing my last hot wing is one way I can love you just as I love myself. I treat you the way I would like to be treated. I can choose to show you love, regardless of what you've done for me or not."

Maeva thought quietly to herself for a minute.

"So, instead of eating all of the candy until my belly is full, I should share some with the other kids. That would be loving!"

"Yes!" said Dad.

"And instead of riding my bike so fast that the others eat my dust, I should ride alongside my friends."

"Exactly."

"Yeah," Maeva said, "I like that. I like how it feels when people are loving to me. I want to make others feel loved, too."

"Hey, you two–what have you been talking about?" Mom asked.

Maeva happily replied, "How love is not just about feeling good but it's about sharing love, just like sharing my favorite cereal, no matter what!"

"That's right, honey! Mom said.

Maeva knew it was true. As they all dug into their favorite cereal, they felt happy and loved.

About the Authors

Both Justin and Alexis are foster care alumni and together, they've traveled to five continents. Among their favorite memories are hiking Table Mountain in South Africa, enjoying ramen in South Korea, and getting engaged in Ecuador. They both enjoy cereal, playing basketball together (Justin often loses to Alexis) and making their daughter Maeva smile. They co-authored a 12-time award-winning, bestselling book titled *Redefining Normal: How Two Foster Kids Beat The Odds and Discovered Healing, Happiness and Love.* Stay tuned for more in the *Maeva and Dad Redefines* kid's book series.